BY JAKE MADDOX

illustrated by Sean Tiffany

text by Bob Temple

Librarian Reviewer
Chris Kreie
Media Specialist, Eden Prairie Schools, MN
MS in Information Media, St. Cloud State University, MN

Reading Consultant
Mary Evenson
Middle School Teacher, Edina Public Schools, MN
MA in Education, University of Minnesota

STONE ARCH BOOKS
Minneapolis   San Diego

Jake Maddox Books are published by Stone Arch Books,
A Capstone Imprint
1710 Roe Crest Drive
North Mankato, Minnesota 56003
www.capstonepub.com

Library of Congress Cataloging-in-Publication Data
Maddox, Jake.
    Backup Goalie / by Jake Maddox; illustrated by Sean Tiffany.
    p. cm. — (Impact Books — A Jake Maddox Sports Story)
    ISBN 978-1-4342-0467-7 (library binding)
    ISBN 978-1-4342-0517-9 (paperback)
    [1. Hockey—Fiction. 2. Leadership—Fiction.] I. Tiffany, Sean, ill.
II. Title.
PZ7.M25643Bac 2008
[Fic]—dc22   2007031259

Summary: Jamie, the captain and star forward of the Comets hockey
team, thinks everything is perfect. His two best friends, Jill and Brett,
are amazing players too. The team is bound for the state championship.
But when Jill is told she can't play on the boys' team anymore, and Brett
is hurt during a match, everything starts to fall apart. To make matters
even worse, Jamie is pulled from his position to fill Brett's place at goal.
Can Jamie make the adjustment and help his team skate to victory — or
are they all on thin ice?

Art Director: Heather Kindseth
Graphic Designer: Kay Fraser

Printed in the United States of America in Stevens Point, Wisconsin.
062013
007584R

TABLE OF CONTENTS

CHAPTER 1

READY TO GO

Jamie bent down and untied his skates. Then he carefully retied both of them, lace by lace. The hockey season was about to start, and Jamie wanted to make sure he was really ready to go.

The Comets' first opponents of the season were already out on the ice getting warmed up, but Jamie's coach kept his team in the locker room for a few extra moments.

"All right, boys," Coach Warren said.

Jamie's friend Jill cleared her throat. Immediately, Coach Warren got an embarrassed look on his face.

The coach quickly corrected himself. "I mean kids," he said. "Sorry, Jill. All right. It's time to hit the ice. The Spartans are going to be a big, physical team. Since this is the first year you are allowed to check in games, I know they will try to use their size to their advantage."

"Yeah, but we've got the speed!" Jamie yelled out.

"That's right," Coach Warren agreed. "We'll need to use our quickness to avoid their checks and to help us score. Let's get out there and go!"

All the players got to their feet at once.

Most of them reached up and snapped their chin straps on their helmets. That made the locker room sound like popcorn popping in a microwave.

Jamie scanned the room.

Just about every player on the team was his size. That meant they weren't nearly big enough to be considered a physical threat on the ice.

The only exception was Brett, the goaltender. He was one of Jamie's best friends, along with Jill.

Brett was the biggest guy in their school. He was nearly a head taller than everyone else. He had a thick, big body, too, so he really blocked the net.

It was tough for the Comets' opponents to get anything past him.

Brett was also one of the quietest kids in school. He was really shy, so he liked wearing the mask and all the padding in goal. It was sort of like wearing a costume.

The faster people tried to fire pucks at Brett, the faster he blocked them and turned them away.

Brett had a great attitude about playing goal. It was a hard position to play, and there was a lot of pressure, but Brett was always calm. He never worried too much about goals he gave up, or anything that had happened in the past.

"I'll stop the next one," is the only thing he would say.

The Comets burst onto the ice and skated around their defensive zone, getting warmed up.

Coach Warren dropped a pile of pucks on the ice, and the players jumped into their pregame routine of drills.

As the Comets' forwards and defense players scooted around the ice, they fired pucks at Brett from all directions.

Brett would flip out a pad here, flash a glove there, or knock the puck to the corner with his stick.

Jamie kept an eye on their opponents, the Spartans, as he warmed up.

The Spartans were huge. Jamie felt like the other guys were twice his size. But as he had expected, they didn't seem as fast as the Comets.

Finally, the horn blared. It was time for the game to start. The Comets gathered around Brett at the goal.

As they always did, the entire Comets team stood together around the net. They crowded in around Brett.

Jamie was the team's captain, so it was his job to say something that would inspire the players.

"Okay, you guys," he said. "They might be bigger than we are, but they can't catch us. And we've got the ultimate big guy in goal. So let's go show them what the Comets are really made of!"

CHAPTER 2
STOP THE NEXT ONE

The Comets broke out of the huddle. Then they skated off toward the bench area.

Most of the players gave Brett's huge leg pads a swat with their sticks for luck before they skated away.

Jamie was last. He and Brett had a special routine they did before each game.

"Hey, big man," Jamie said, just like always.

He skated around Brett as he talked.

"What are you gonna do?" Jamie yelled.

Jamie always hoped Brett would yell the next line. But he always just spoke it, calmly and quietly.

"Stop the next one," Brett said.

"And after that?" Jamie barked back.

"Stop the next one," Brett said.

As the referee's whistle blew, Jamie spun around in front of Brett and swung his stick at Brett's leg pads.

The pads thundered. *Thooomb!*

Brett didn't move an inch.

Jamie whizzed out to center ice. As the center on the first line, he would take the opening face-off.

Jill was the right wing on Jamie's line. A player named Marcus was the left wing.

Jill and Jamie had played on a line together since their second year in hockey.

The first year, Jamie played in goal. He struggled with the position, and he longed for a chance to use his speed.

Then Brett moved to town and wanted to play goalie. Jamie was more than willing to give it up.

Jamie had found his perfect position at center. Jamie led the team in assists almost every season. Either he or Jill always led the team in goals.

Jill had grown up playing with the boys, and she was one of the best players in the league. She kept playing with the boys even after a girls' program was started.

This year, since checking was allowed, Jill's parents had wanted to put her in the girls' league instead. They were worried that Jill would get hurt.

But Jill didn't want to switch to the girls' team. Plus, because of funding cutbacks, this year there were only two girls' teams. One was for girls ages 12 and under, and one was for girls ages 16–18. There wasn't anything for Jill, who was 14. So she ended up staying on the boys' team.

For five years, Jamie, Jill, and Brett had dominated the South Central League. The Comets had won the league championship every season. They had won the regional championship twice.

They had even gone to the state tournament and done well, too.

Their goal was to win the state championship. They felt that this could be the year.

Just as the referee got ready to drop the puck to start the season, there was a bunch of noise behind the Spartans' bench.

The Spartans' coach was yelling at the referee. The coach was waving some kind of booklet in his hand. He looked mad.

The referee skated over toward the Spartans' bench. As team captain, Jamie skated with him.

"I'm sorry, sir," the Spartans' coach said, "but is that a girl out there?"

He said "girl" like it was some kind of a bad word, Jamie thought.

Everyone looked out at Jill.

"Yeah, she's a girl," Jamie said.

"Well, I'm sorry, son, but she can't play in this game," the Spartans' coach said. He pointed at the booklet he held and added, "It says so right here."

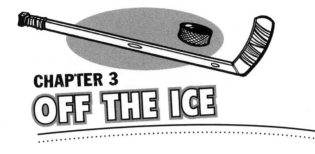

CHAPTER 3

OFF THE ICE

The referee grabbed the booklet and opened it. Jamie read the cover: "The Official Rules of the City South Central Boys' Hockey League." The referee flipped through the pages.

"Here we go, Rule 7," the referee said. "Female players shall only be allowed to play if there is no girls' team available for them in the City South Central Girls' Hockey League."

By then, Coach Warren had gotten close enough to hear the conversation.

"That's right," he yelled. "That's the rule. And there's no Comets girls' team at her age level, so she's allowed to play with us."

The Spartans' coach was getting worked up. "But there are other girls' teams. And there are teams in the other leagues and in other cities that she could play on," he said. "It doesn't have to be a team here."

All the adults looked at each other. No one was sure what to do.

Jamie knew what he wanted to do, though. "Let's play hockey," he said. "You guys can figure this out later."

Seeing the adults arguing near the bench, the league's commissioner worked his way down to the ice.

The referee explained the problem and the commissioner looked a little confused.

"This is a new rule," he said slowly, "and I can see that it can be interpreted a couple of different ways. It's not very clear. I think for the time being, she should be held out of games. We need to sort this out." The commissioner crossed his arms.

Jamie groaned. He turned and skated out to Jill. He told her what was happening. Jill's head drooped.

As tough as she looked wearing full hockey gear, she looked like she might start to cry.

Jamie put his arm around her as they skated off the ice. "Don't worry, you'll be back before you know it," Jamie said. "They can't keep you away from the Comets!"

He wasn't so sure, but he wanted Jill to feel better. "And in the meantime," he added, "we'll win this game for you."

Coach Warren put Danny out to take Jill's place at right wing. Finally, they were ready for the game to start.

The referee dropped the puck.

Jamie and the Spartans' center jostled for it. Jamie pulled it free and dropped it back to a defenseman. The Spartans' center knocked Jamie to the ice with a bump.

Jamie scrambled back to his feet, wheeled around, and headed to the offensive zone.

The defenseman tried to feed the puck to Danny, but a Spartans forward intercepted it. They raced in on Brett and got off a quick shot. Brett turned it away with a pad.

The puck bounced to the corner. A Comets defenseman tried to get it, but a Spartans winger pulled it away. He centered it out front.

Jamie blocked the pass, but it deflected to a Spartan at the point.

For the next minute, the Spartans dominated the ice.

Brett made save after save, but the big Spartans team just kept coming.

Finally, the puck rolled to the corner. Jamie and the rest of the Comets were tired. They needed a line change. But with the puck in their end, they couldn't switch. They needed to force a face-off.

A Comets defenseman was battling for the puck in the corner. "Tie it up!" Jamie yelled. But the puck came free.

Again, it was fed out into the slot. Jamie tried to check the Spartans' center coming down the slot, but he was too big for Jamie to handle.

As they battled for position, they both lost their balance. They slid hard into Brett, and the puck sailed harmlessly away.

That's when Brett made a noise Jamie had never heard before.

Brett crumpled to the ground. His knee was bent to one side.

Jamie looked down. He saw that his friend was lying on the ice. Brett was screaming in pain.

CHAPTER 4
GO IN GOAL

Jamie and a couple other players helped Brett off the ice. Brett couldn't put any weight on his left leg.

Jamie couldn't believe what had happened to his day.

When he woke up that morning, he had been full of excitement. The Comets had another chance to win the Central League. They could make a run for the state championship.

Now, in less than five minutes, he had lost two of the team's best players and his two best friends on the team. Maybe even for the whole season. Everything had come crashing down around him.

When he got back to the bench after helping Brett to the locker room, Jamie's day got even worse.

"Jamie," Coach Warren said, "I need you to go in goal."

"Me?" Jamie exclaimed. "Are you kidding? What about Carlos?" Jamie knew they had another goalie. But then he realized he hadn't seen Carlos that day.

"Carlos is having trouble with his grades," the coach replied. "He's out for the semester. And you're the only one on the team who has played goalie before."

"But Coach, that was years ago!" Jamie said.

"Jamie, I need you in goal," the coach said again. His voice was firmer this time. "Go put on the equipment."

Jamie turned and went to the locker room.

The game was held up while he worked his way into the 30 pounds of equipment that Brett wore in goal.

The hardest part wasn't the weight of the gear. It was the size.

Brett's leg pads were huge on Jamie. The chest protector hung off Jamie's sides. He could barely move.

"This is ridiculous," Jamie muttered as he stood up to head back to the rink.

Brett already had a big bag of ice on his left knee. His father was there, getting ready to take him to the hospital for X-rays.

Jamie headed back to the ice. "Hey, Jamie," Brett called. "Stop the next one."

Jamie smiled. "Got it," he said. "Stop the next one."

But Jamie didn't feel like he could stop anything wearing all that equipment. He stumbled out to the ice and made his way to the goal crease.

That's when one of the Comets' defensemen came up. He whacked Jamie's leg pads, yelling, "Stop the next one!"

Unlike Brett, who always stood firm, Jamie crumpled to the ground. As he fought his way back to his feet, he heard some people in the crowd laughing.

Finally, the referee dropped the puck to start the game.

To Jamie, the game seemed to last forever.

He did his best to get in front of the pucks the Spartans shot. But in that huge equipment, it was really hard to move.

So, if the puck was shot right at him, he stopped it. If it was off to one side or another, he had no chance.

By the end of the game, the Spartans had put six goals behind Jamie.

Without Jamie and Jill on offense, the Comets managed only one goal. The season began with a 6–1 loss.

Jamie stormed off the ice. He yanked off the goalie equipment in the locker room. He was mad.

After each game, Coach Warren gave the team some pointers.

Today, he wrapped up his talk by saying a nice thing about Jamie. "That wasn't easy, going in goal like that," the coach said. "We should all thank Jamie for trying so hard."

Whew, Jamie thought. At least I don't have to do that again.

But Coach Warren had different ideas. "Jamie, come talk to me before you leave," he said.

CHAPTER 5

STEP UP

Jamie knew what the coach wanted to talk about. He just knew Coach Warren wanted him to go in goal again during the next game.

"Jamie, we're going to need you to play in goal until Brett gets back," Coach Warren said. "I hope that won't be long, but we need a good player in there."

Jamie sighed. Great. Now his day couldn't get any worse.

"But Coach, how are we going to score any goals without me and Jill at forward?" Jamie asked. "Wouldn't it be better to put someone else in goal, and keep me up on offense?"

Coach Warren wasn't about to budge. "Jamie, you're our captain," the coach said. "Without Brett and Jill, we're going to struggle. You and I both know that. But the rest of the team needs to believe that we can win. I need you to step up and be the leader of this team."

Jamie didn't know what to say.

He wanted to say the right thing, which was that he would do his best in goal and try to help his teammates.

But scoring goals was his favorite part of the game.

And if he was playing goalie, he wasn't going to do any scoring at all.

But he had to do what his coach said. So Jamie nodded at Coach Warren and turned to leave. "See you at practice," Jamie said.

CHAPTER 6
MORE BAD NEWS

When Jamie showed up at practice the next night, Coach Warren had a surprise for him.

"I borrowed a set of goalie equipment from a different team. I think it will fit you a little bit better," the coach said. "That should make your job as goalie easier."

Jamie found that the coach was right. The equipment did fit better. It was much lighter, too.

That allowed Jamie to move better and more quickly, so he could get to more shots. And getting to more shots meant he was able to stop more shots.

Still, Jamie had a hard time during practice. The main reason he didn't let in many goals was that the shooters weren't doing a very good job.

Two nights later, the Comets were scheduled to play their second game of the season. This time, they would face the Badgers.

The Badgers were an average team in the league. The Comets usually beat them easily. The year before, they'd won by six points. But because of the Comets' new lineup and missing players, Jamie knew this year's game would be tough.

He wasn't looking forward to the game at all.

* * *

The day of the game, Jamie got some more bad news.

Jill stopped at his house after school to tell him what was going on. They didn't have any classes together, so she hadn't had a chance to talk to him during the day.

They sat in Jamie's room with sodas. "So, what's the scoop?" Jamie asked.

Jill sighed. "They aren't going to talk about it until the next board meeting, and that's two weeks from now," she said. "So until then, they put me on the Spartans' girls team. Can you believe that? Me, a Spartan?"

Jamie shook his head in disbelief.

"We don't have practice tonight, so I can come to your game," Jill said. "Brett's going to come too. Did you hear what the doctor said about his knee?"

"Oh, no," Jamie said, fearing the worst. "Not more bad news."

CHAPTER 7
NO CHANCE

Jamie braced himself for what he was about to hear.

"Brett's knee is sprained really bad," Jill said. "He can use crutches to walk, but I guess he's not going to be able to play for two or three months."

"Two or three months?" Jamie exclaimed. "That's more than half the season! I can't stay in goal that long!" He couldn't believe it.

"Come on, Jamie," Jill said, trying to sound encouraging. "It won't be so bad. All you have to do is win enough games to keep us in the running for the playoffs. Even if you only win half the games, we'll be okay by the time Brett and I get back."

Jamie didn't care. "Are you kidding me?" he yelled. "In two or three months, we'll be something like 0–20. Even if Wayne Gretzky came to play for us, we wouldn't have a chance!"

Jill laughed. She knew Jamie was being his usual nervous self. He was just imagining the worst that could happen.

"Just stop the next one," she said, laughing. "And then the one after that, too!"

of Your Junior League Hockey News

Hockey News

Tuesday, October 28 $1.00

Comets Worst Team EVER

Losers, Losers, Losers!
by Peggy Dunbar

It's all Jamie Link's fault. That's the word around the league as to why the Comets, who only one year ago went on to win the Excel Cup, are now at the bottom of the league with no chance of digging their way out.

It all started with the Comets losing their head goaltender, Brett Morgan, to an injury in the first game of the season. They also lost Jill Tanaka to a new league rule that has yet to be resolved. Jamie Link, the Comets lead forward and team captain, reluctantly stepped into goal...

...e of Link, ...e Comet's ...o almost ...ce in net ...team in

a Streak!
Graf
...e off to
...year as
...ry team
...r way.
...says he's
...the team
...says he
...y they
...all the
...Excel
...on.

...Mills
...e
...o out
...est",
...hat
...the
...n so
...vins

...ut

Not only are the Comets the worst team in the South Central League this year but they just... the WORST TEAM EVER! If Team Cap... new Goal Tender Jamie Link can't turn i... around the Comets are destined to fa... everything they try in life.

everything they try in lif...

...around the Comets are de...
everything they t...

around the Comets...
everything t...

new Goal Tender J...
around the Cor...

- 43 -

CHAPTER 8
BAD ATTITUDE

That night, when Jamie showed up for the game, he was in a terrible mood.

Usually, before a game, he was excited. He would laugh a lot, tell jokes, and get everyone else on the team excited too.

That night was different. Jamie wasn't excited. He got dressed quickly, slamming his locker door and stomping around.

He was a real grump.

He grumbled as he put on his equipment. He whined as he did his stretching exercises. He growled as the team warmed up for the game.

Finally, the puck dropped to start the action. Jamie tried his best to focus.

But then the Badgers' first shot of the game snuck past him. It sailed between him and the left post for the game's first goal. The Badgers were already in the lead.

Jamie's attitude took an even deeper dive after that happened.

"This stinks!" he yelled out loud.

He slammed his stick against one of the goal posts. Then he yelled, "We don't have a chance!"

The rest of the game wasn't much better.

Jamie played better than he had in the game against the Spartans, but he still let four goals get past him.

Worse, the Comets offense couldn't put any pressure on the Badgers' net.

It was a total loss, 4–0.

Jamie couldn't remember the last time the Comets had gone an entire game without scoring a goal.

He wasn't sure it had ever happened.

After the game, Jamie didn't say a word to Jill and Brett, who had come to watch. He bolted straight from the arena and headed home.

At home, Jamie showered quickly and got into his pajamas.

All he wanted to do was close his eyes.

Jamie just wanted to forget about hockey for a while.

But before he got into bed, he heard the chime of his doorbell. A moment later, he heard his mother call, "Jamie, your friends are here."

Jamie's bedroom door swung open. Brett hobbled in on crutches. Jill was right behind him.

"Can you believe that game?" Jamie blurted out. He was feeling very sorry for himself. "Wasn't that awful?"

"Yeah, it stunk," Brett said.

Jill agreed. "Yep, terrible," she said. "And we think the worst part of the whole game was you."

CHAPTER 9
A NEW JAMIE?

Jamie wasn't sure what his friends meant.

Were they saying he was a terrible goalie? No matter what they meant, he was sure it wasn't good.

"Yeah, I didn't play very well," Jamie mumbled.

"Oh, it wasn't that," Jill said. "We actually think you played fine."

Jamie looked up. Brett nodded at him.

"It's your attitude that stinks," Jill said.

Jamie really wasn't sure what to do or say. He could feel himself getting very mad.

"What am I supposed to do?" he yelled angrily. "I'm playing a position I hate, and our team stinks. Before, we were a team that could have won the state tournament. Now we're a team that can't even score a single goal."

"I thought you were the captain of the team," Jill said.

"I am the captain," Jamie said.

"You're not acting like it," Jill said. "You're supposed to be helping everyone get better, not yelling and whining just because things got a little hard."

Jamie felt like his friends were attacking him. "What about you, Jill?" he said, crossing his arms and looking at Jill. "You came over and whined about playing for the Spartans girls' team."

"That's when I'm with you guys, in private," Jill said, shaking her head. "It's one thing to talk to your friends. It's another thing to take that to the game. That hurts your own team. When I'm with the Spartans girls, I try my best and don't complain. You're making us all look bad out there."

The room was quiet for a long time.

Finally, Brett spoke up. "We're still a team," he said to Jamie. "Jill and I aren't playing now, but that doesn't mean we're not Comets. When we get back, we want the team to still be together!"

Jamie looked at his friends. He suddenly felt very bad about the way he had acted.

But at the same time, Jamie felt a sense of pride. They were all still Comets. And it was up to Jamie to keep the team moving forward.

"Okay, I get it," Jamie finally said. "From now on, you'll see a new Jamie."

Jill and Brett laughed. "I can't wait to meet him," Jill said.

CHAPTER 10
CAPTAIN

The next night at practice, Jamie showed up with a smile on his face.

He walked right over to Coach Warren and asked if he could talk to him.

"Hey, Coach," Jamie said. "I brought my regular skates. I was thinking I could skate out tonight."

"No, Jamie," Coach Warren began. "You know we need you in goal until Brett gets back."

Jamie smiled. "I know, Coach," he said. "I've got an idea. For the first half of practice, let me skate out with the forwards. I can help them with handling the puck, and passing and shooting drills. Plus, that will give me a chance to keep my forward skills sharp for when Brett gets back."

Coach Warren's eyes lit up. It looked like he was beginning to like this idea.

"Then, for the second half of practice, I'll put the goalie gear on and work on my goaltending, and the forwards can shoot at a real goalie," Jamie said.

Coach Warren beamed. "That's the kind of thinking I like in a captain," he said. "Go ahead and get ready."

Score one for the new Jamie, Jamie thought as he put on his equipment.

Once the ice was ready for play, Jamie was the first player on it. When the rest of the team joined him, he led stretching exercises. He also filled the other players in on his plan for that night's practice.

When drills began, it seemed like Jamie was everywhere.

One minute he was skating to the net and making a great play of his own. The next minute he was explaining positions to a teammate or helping another with his passing.

Halfway through practice, Jamie skated off to change into his goalie gear. When he came back on, the smile was still on his face.

Even in goal, he was encouraging his teammates and calling out instructions.

Coach Warren barely had to say a word the whole practice.

The Comets' fortunes began to change almost right away. In the first game back, they scored three goals against the Muskies.

They lost the game 4–3, but the whole team left the ice feeling better.

The game after that, Jill and Brett came to watch. Jill carried a sign that read, "Go Comets! Go Jamie!"

Jamie smiled when he saw it.

That night, he had his best game yet in goal. He made 26 saves. The Comets tied the Bruins, ending up 2–2.

CHAPTER 11
LIKE OLD TIMES

Over the course of the next few weeks, the Comets kept getting better.

They won two games, tied two, and only lost one.

That left them with a record of two wins, four losses, and three ties heading into a rematch with the Spartans.

The night before the Spartans game, Jamie's phone rang.

"May I speak to the Comets' star goalie?" Jill said, laughing into the phone.

"Knock it off, Jill," Jamie said. But he smiled.

"Hey, guess what?" Jill said. She sounded happy. "I've got some good news for you. As of today, I'm a Comet again!"

Jill explained that after lots of arguing, the league's board voted to let her play for the Comets boys' team.

They finally agreed because she had been registered to play with the Comets, and there was no Comets girls' team at her age level.

When Jill returned to the Comets, she helped the team turn the corner. The rest of the forwards had already started to play a lot better.

Jill stepped right into the first line with Marcus and Danny. The three teammates clicked right away.

By the end of January, Brett's knee was healthy enough for him to return.

The Comets were right where they hoped they would be. They had ten wins, nine losses, and five ties.

Jamie was ready to jump right back in at forward, since he had been practicing all along.

Jamie showed up early for his first game back at forward. Then he looked at the lines Coach Warren had posted on the locker room wall.

He saw that his name was listed at center on the first line. Jill would be on his right, just like old times.

But Jamie had one more surprise for Coach Warren and the team.

"Hey Coach," Jamie said. "Why don't you put me on the second or third line? Jill's line has been doing great. I don't want to screw it up. Plus, then we'll have two good scoring lines."

"Still thinking like a captain, I see," said Coach Warren, smiling.

The coach made the switch. During the game that night, each line scored two goals.

A few months later, it was time for the Comets to accept their state championship trophy. And it was their captain, Jamie, who got his hands on it first.

ABOUT THE AUTHOR

Bob Temple lives in Rosemount, Minnesota, with his wife and three children. He has written more than thirty books for children. Over the years, he has coached more than twenty kids' soccer, basketball, and baseball teams. He also loves visiting classrooms to talk about his writing.

ABOUT THE ILLUSTRATOR

When Sean Tiffany was growing up, he lived on a small island off the coast of Maine. Every day, from sixth grade until he graduated from high school, he had to take a boat to get to school. When Sean isn't working on his art, he works on a multimedia project called "OilCan Drive," which combines music and art. He has a pet cactus named Jim.

GLOSSARY

advantage (ad-VAN-tij)—something that helps you or is useful to you

blared (BLAIRD)—made a loud and unpleasant noise

commissioner (kuh-MISH-uhn-ur)—the person in charge of a sport or league

crutches (KRUHTCH-iz)—supports that fit under the armpits and help an injured person walk

cutbacks (KUHT-baks)—when money given to an organization is taken away or reduced

funding (FUHN-ding)—money given to an organization

hobble (HOB-uhl)—to walk with difficulty because you are in pain or are injured

pressure (PRESH-ur)—a burden or strain

sprained (SPRAYND)—injured a joint by twisting or tearing its muscles or ligaments

threat (THRET)—a person or group regarded as a danger

ultimate (UHL-tuh-mit)—greatest or best

MORE ABOUT
USA HOCKEY

USA Hockey is the national governing body for hockey in the United States. It puts together the national teams for men's and women's hockey. These are the teams that end up playing in the Olympic Games.

USA Hockey is also in charge of most amateur hockey in America, including youth leagues.

At the end of every season, youth teams can play in district tournaments all around the United States. The winners of these tournaments play in the national tournaments, which are held each spring. National championships are awarded at every age level, for both boys and girls.

In addition to organizing the national championships, USA Hockey also works to promote fair play at all levels. It tries to get more players interested in playing hockey.

HOCKEY WORDS
YOU SHOULD KNOW

championship (CHAM-pee-uhn-ship)—a contest that determines which team will win

check (CHEK)—in hockey, to stop someone with one's body or stick

drill (DRIL)—a way to learn something by doing it over and over

forward (FOR-wurd)— player who has an attacking position and tries to score goals

goaltender (GOHL-ten-dur)—the person who tries to keep the puck from entering the goal

intercepted (in-tur-SEPT-id)—stopped the movement of something

league (LEEG)—a group of sports teams that share the same rules

opponent (uh-POH-nuhnt)—someone who is against you in a game

puck (PUHK)—the hard, round piece of rubber used in hockey

referee (ref-uh-REE)—someone who supervises a sports match or game and makes sure the rules are obeyed

DISCUSSION QUESTIONS

1. Why did Jill want to stay on the boys'
   team? Do you think boys and girls
   should be allowed to be on the same
   teams? Talk about it.

2. When Jamie has to play goalie, he
   develops a very bad attitude. Have you
   ever had to do something you didn't
   want to do? How did you handle it? Talk
   about your experience.

3. What do you think are the most
   important things for a captain of a team
   to do? How should a captain act?

WRITING PROMPTS

1. At the end of this book, we find out that Jamie and his team have won the state championship. What do you think happened during that game? Write about it!

2. Brett sprained his leg during this book and couldn't play. Have you ever had to sit out from your favorite sport? Why did you have to? How did you pass the time while you couldn't play? Write about it.

3. When Jamie acts grumpy, his friends help him snap out of it. Have you ever seen a friend in a similar situation? What did you do to help? Write about ways you can help friends develop better attitudes.

OTHER BOOKS

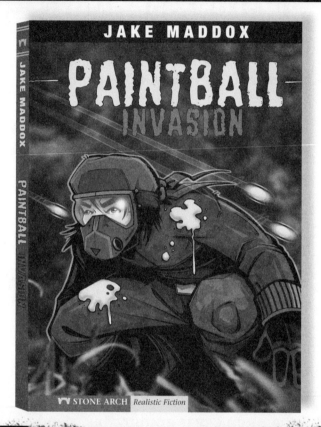

JAKE MADDOX

PAINTBALL
INVASION

STONE ARCH *Realistic Fiction*

Josh and Chad have been using the same place as a paintball field forever. But now, someone's attacking them. Who's out to stop their paintballing fun? It's going to take all the skills they have to stop the sabotage.